Unspoken Promises

Hatty Jones

Published by Hatty Jones, 2024.

This is a work of fiction. Similarities to real people, places, or events are entirely coincidental.

UNSPOKEN PROMISES

First edition. October 25, 2024.

Copyright © 2024 Hatty Jones.

ISBN: 979-8224653652

Written by Hatty Jones.

Unspoken Promises

In the spaces between our words, in the quiet moments when eyes meet, hands linger, or a fleeting smile escapes, unspoken promises are made. They're the silent vows woven into the fabric of our lives—commitments we don't always vocalize, yet feel deeply in our hearts. They exist in the pauses between sentences, the spaces in our breaths, and the rhythms of our daily lives. They define who we are to others, and, perhaps more profoundly, who we are to ourselves.

This collection of poems delves into these quiet covenants. Each piece is a tribute to the subtle, often overlooked moments that shape our relationships, our growth, and our sense of belonging. From the tender understanding shared between friends to the unexpressed vows of love, from silent pacts with nature to the internal promises that push us forward, Unspoken Promises celebrates the power of the unsaid. These poems are here to explore what we feel but can't always articulate—the words we carry silently, as they shape our lives with profound purpose and delicate strength.

As you turn these pages, I invite you to reflect on your own silent promises, the ones tucked within memories, shared glances, and inner resolve. May these words give voice to those quiet commitments and remind us that sometimes, the things we leave unsaid speak the loudest.

Love & Relationships

Unvoiced Echoes

In the room where silence lingers long,
Words unsaid hang heavy, sharp and still,
Our voices quiver, tied by doubt's strong song,
Each heart beat swells with what we dare not spill.
Through clenched and quiet breath, our love is bound,
Yet tangled up in fears we never name,
An ache, a longing, pulses all around,
What could have blossomed wilts, untouched by flame.
If only we had braved the words unsaid,
Dared to let our fears and passions meet,
Perhaps the silence now would ease its dread,
And soften where our silent sorrows beat.
But here we sit, our echoes locked away,
What might have lived, we bury in delay.

The Silence Between Us

There's a gulf we crafted, silent and wide,
Where words drifted off, too timid to stay,
Beneath our smiles, our gazes side by side,
Lie questions and truths we've kept far at bay.
A sigh replaces what we long to ask,
A glance conveys what lips cannot reveal,
We wear brave faces, keeping on the mask,
Yet silence wounds, a hurt we do not heal.
These words we hoard for fear of what they'll change,
Lay dormant, like seeds that never find earth,
Though whispered thoughts could shift what feels so strange,
We let them die, withholding their true worth.
In silence we stand, shadows of what's real,
Afraid to share the depths of what we feel.

Love's Unspoken Weight

Beneath the gaze, so tender yet restrained,
A thousand words collect, yet never fly,
In quiet pain, the heart stays uncomplained,
And holds the secrets we let slowly die.
What harm in voicing love so deeply felt?
What fear holds captive truths we should convey?
Instead, this silence tightens, steel and belt,
An anchor dropped in what we will not say.
Your eyes find mine, a flicker then withdraws,
The ache of what we know yet do not dare—
In love's great reach, there lives a quiet clause,
That words might spoil what silence built with care.
But silence too can wound and break apart,
Unspoken weights lay heavy on the heart.

Buried Beneath a Smile

A laugh, a smile, a practiced, light façade,
To keep the truth concealed, yet aching still,
Behind the ease, our guarded hearts applaud,
Refusing to let words break through our will.
And in this silence blooms a quiet strife,
For words could heal or shatter what remains,
Yet here we hold our separate lives in life,
In fear that what we share may bring us pain.
Our smiles grow hollow, buried under lies,
With layers thick, we dare not even peek,
To see the truth in one another's eyes—
A truth we're too afraid to let us speak.
So here we stay, in laughter's thin disguise,
And leave our love beneath a mask of sighs.

The Pause that Lingers

A breath, a pause, a moment split in two,
Where all the unsaid things begin to wait,
Suspended in the air, untried, untrue,
Caught up in fear that silence could abate.
For silence here feels safer than the truth,
In knowing that the words might risk goodbye,
We linger in this stillness, bound in youth,
While years slip by, and bolder feelings die.
The ache of words we've kept beneath the skin,
A distant dream we dare not bring to light,
If spoken, might break open, not within,
But still we pause, and withhold what feels right.
And so we stay, in tension and regret,
As dreams remain in silence, unmet yet.

Ghosts of What We Left Unsaid

Each unvoiced thought a ghost that haunts the room,
A shadowed wraith of words we dared not share,
In silence, they return to us in gloom,
Refusing to let go, still hanging there.
If only we had braved the brittle speech,
If only we had voiced our hopes and fears,
Perhaps love's fullest light we might have reached,
Instead of clinging to these ghostly tears.
Now, every glance contains a muted cry,
Of could-have-beens and echoes left unclaimed,
Our quiet past lies thick with hollow sighs,
Each silence speaks the pain we never named.
These ghosts remain, a burdened, heavy chain,
The price we pay for love we could not sustain.

Promises in Passing

In the early light, a gentle nod,
the quiet touch of a hand against mine,
a vow we never spoke but knew—
to return, to be here when it mattered.
These moments echo, soft but steady,
held together by the weight of silence.
Long after the touch fades, the nod forgotten,
the promise lingers, woven into memory.
Even in our distance, across years,
those brief, quiet moments surface,
as if to remind me—
of what we knew without saying.
These are not promises to keep,
not vows with words or boundaries,
yet somehow they stay,
shaping the silence between us.

Unfading Murmurs

There was no need for words then,
we understood in breaths and glances,
in the way we shared a space,
in the rhythm of being there together.
Promises born of patience, of waiting,
unspoken yet clear as the quiet sky.
Even now, I feel their gentle pull,
a murmur I carry, soft as dusk.
The echo of that evening sits with me still,
the way we watched the world grow dark,
the unspoken agreement to hold,
to be held, even in silence.
It remains, an unfading whisper,
a promise without edges or end,
yet I feel it, real as any word—
the lasting weight of all we left unsaid.

Moments Without Sound

In that narrow space between words,
we made our pact—
not with language or vows,
but with a shared glance across the room.
In the silence, something rooted,
a promise that would not fade,
though neither of us spoke it.
It held, it stayed, in the absence of sound.
Years on, I remember the softness,
that silent commitment like a touch,
a promise that nothing could erode.
It lives between breaths, in stillness.
Sometimes, I wonder if you feel it, too—
the echo of that quiet promise,
a bond we left unspoken,
yet carry forward, still and deep.

In the Space Between

There was a way we looked then,
a kind of calm resolve,
as if both of us knew—
without saying—what we meant to keep.
Our promises were gentle, silent things,
unannounced, without demands,
yet they settled into place,
formed of nothing but the space between us.
Even now, across years and miles,
they echo back, clear as day.
The words we didn't need then
still hover, solid and sure.
This promise wasn't a thing to break,
but a quiet vow to carry forward,
a steady presence, wordless and vast,
keeping its own place, its own meaning.

Weight of Quiet Promises

Underneath the stars, we spoke in silence,
a language only we understood—
promises too delicate for words,
held close in that soft light.
They lingered, echoing long after,
like threads woven into time,
binding us not with vows spoken aloud
but with something deeper, felt.
Those moments became anchors,
keeping us steady, apart or together,
a promise that distance couldn't touch,
a memory we could return to.
Now, in quiet moments alone,
I hear them, those faint echoes,
as if each breath brings back that night,
the weight of a promise still alive.

An Oath in Silence

The world faded in those quiet hours,
and we sat together, understanding,
though not a word was said.
Our voices stilled, yet promises grew.
They were not binding, these vows,
nor were they fragile things to shatter.
They found their place in the quiet,
formed of glances, of simple gestures.
Years drift by, but the silence remains,
an echo I feel more than hear.
Our promise sits there, soft yet solid,
a presence in the spaces between days.
Even when we part, I sense its weight,
a quiet comfort, a familiar call.
An oath not to be broken,
though never spoken aloud.

Promises in Passing

In the early light, a gentle nod,
the quiet touch of a hand against mine,
a vow we never spoke but knew—
to return, to be here when it mattered.
These moments echo, soft but steady,
held together by the weight of silence.
Long after the touch fades, the nod forgotten,
the promise lingers, woven into memory.
Even in our distance, across years,
those brief, quiet moments surface,
as if to remind me—
of what we knew without saying.
These are not promises to keep,
not vows with words or boundaries,
yet somehow they stay,
shaping the silence between us.

Unfading Murmurs

There was no need for words then,
we understood in breaths and glances,
in the way we shared a space,
in the rhythm of being there together.
Promises born of patience, of waiting,
unspoken yet clear as the quiet sky.
Even now, I feel their gentle pull,
a murmur I carry, soft as dusk.
The echo of that evening sits with me still,
the way we watched the world grow dark,
the unspoken agreement to hold,
to be held, even in silence.
It remains, an unfading whisper,
a promise without edges or end,
yet I feel it, real as any word—
the lasting weight of all we left unsaid.

Moments Without Sound

In that narrow space between words,
we made our pact—
not with language or vows,
but with a shared glance across the room.
In the silence, something rooted,
a promise that would not fade,
though neither of us spoke it.
It held, it stayed, in the absence of sound.
Years on, I remember the softness,
that silent commitment like a touch,
a promise that nothing could erode.
It lives between breaths, in stillness.
Sometimes, I wonder if you feel it, too—
the echo of that quiet promise,
a bond we left unspoken,
yet carry forward, still and deep.

In the Space Between

There was a way we looked then,
a kind of calm resolve,
as if both of us knew—
without saying—what we meant to keep.
Our promises were gentle, silent things,
unannounced, without demands,
yet they settled into place,
formed of nothing but the space between us.
Even now, across years and miles,
they echo back, clear as day.
The words we didn't need then
still hover, solid and sure.
This promise wasn't a thing to break,
but a quiet vow to carry forward,
a steady presence, wordless and vast,
keeping its own place, its own meaning.

Weight of Quiet Promises

Underneath the stars, we spoke in silence,
a language only we understood—
promises too delicate for words,
held close in that soft light.
They lingered, echoing long after,
like threads woven into time,
binding us not with vows spoken aloud
but with something deeper, felt.
Those moments became anchors,
keeping us steady, apart or together,
a promise that distance couldn't touch,
a memory we could return to.
Now, in quiet moments alone,
I hear them, those faint echoes,
as if each breath brings back that night,
the weight of a promise still alive.

An Oath in Silence

The world faded in those quiet hours,
and we sat together, understanding,
though not a word was said.
Our voices stilled, yet promises grew.
They were not binding, these vows,
nor were they fragile things to shatter.
They found their place in the quiet,
formed of glances, of simple gestures.
Years drift by, but the silence remains,
an echo I feel more than hear.
Our promise sits there, soft yet solid,
a presence in the spaces between days.
Even when we part, I sense its weight,
a quiet comfort, a familiar call.
An oath not to be broken,
though never spoken aloud.

A Promise in Stillness

I wait in the quiet of this room,
footsteps and voices fading behind,
holding steady as hours stretch long.
This space becomes a promise,
each minute a vow to remain,
to be here when you cross back.
The air thickens with memory,
with the sound of your voice,
the faint trace of your laugh.
I stay, anchored in the waiting,
trusting the pull of your return,
holding the door open, still.

Breath Held, Unspoken

In the pause of breath, a promise waits—
soft, invisible, yet unwavering,
settling like dust across the floor.
I am here, keeping still,
as if you might return at any moment,
as if my staying could call you back.
I wait, an act of quiet faith,
my presence the only proof
that I believe in what we hold.
Outside, the world keeps moving,
but here, I remain, unspoken,
held fast in the hope of your return.

An Open Door

This threshold is a line drawn soft,
a place between your leaving and return,
where I stand, faithful in the quiet.
Each second whispers promises—
to be here when you cross it again,
to hold the silence until it breaks.
There's no rush in this waiting,
no hurried breath, no restless hands,
just the steady trust in what we are.
I keep the door wide open,
as if it alone could lead you home,
as if love's patience were enough.

The Shape of Absence

Your absence fills this space,
yet I stand here, still, a silent vow,
a steady point in shifting light.
What I hold isn't fragile,
though it trembles in each heartbeat,
a quiet promise to wait.
The threshold becomes my world,
where memory and hope meet,
blurring where you are and where you'll be.
I wait, unshaken by time,
rooted by all we shared,
trusting that you will return.

Holding Time

Time stretches thin in waiting,
each minute a small prayer,
a promise etched in quiet resolve.
In the stillness, I feel you near,
as if my patience could reach out,
calling you home with every breath.
This waiting is its own language,
a silent song, steady and soft,
filling the space you left behind.
So I hold, unmoving, open-armed,
the threshold a line to be crossed,
a promise held by the weight of hope.

Faith in the Empty Space

The empty space becomes my vigil,
a place where faith is nurtured,
quiet, calm, unwavering.
I sit, waiting for the sound of you,
for the familiar touch of presence,
for the air to shift as you walk in.
This waiting is a silent bond,
a vow I make to you alone,
a promise bound in patience.
The threshold waits with me,
a quiet, steady keeper of hope,
where absence gives way to return.

Invisible Threads

In the hush between words, we find our way,
building something beyond what voices make.
Our bridge is woven from looks and small gestures,
a silent language that needs no reply.
Time has taught us to read in gentle pauses,
to sense what each heart carries quietly.
We do not speak each vow, yet they linger,
soft as the breath that rests between our words.
With each year, the silence grows more alive,
a place where our promises settle in peace.
The spaces between us draw us closer,
as trust blooms in all we do not say.
This bridge endures without stone or steel,
stronger than words, woven by what we feel.

Unseen Foundations

There are promises built not in sound,
but in the patient holding of silence,
in the way we sit, side by side,
knowing words are not always the answer.
Over time, this silence has taken shape,
a foundation we lean on without fear.
It is not emptiness, but shared presence,
a quiet strength that holds us in place.
Each pause becomes a thread, woven gently,
binding us with all that's left unsaid.
We understand beyond spoken language,
finding solace in what we cannot name.
Our bridge is silent yet enduring,
unseen but trusted, deep and assuring.

What Lies Beneath

Underneath each smile, each look we share,
there lives a silent vow, steady and true.
We don't always need the weight of words
to know what lies beneath, quietly held.
With time, we've come to trust this silence,
to know it speaks of things far deeper still.
Our bond grows in these moments unspoken,
where peace settles in unvoiced promises.
It's here that love finds its lasting shape,
not in loud declarations, but calm.
We understand the bridge we've built together,
steady beneath us, quiet and strong.
It holds us without the need for sound,
a promise built on solid, silent ground.

Beyond Words

Our language is a bridge we've learned to cross,
built on trust and unspoken acceptance,
knowing that words are not always needed
to carry the weight of what we hold close.
Over the years, our silence has grown sure,
a way to understand without saying,
to stand together in quiet moments,
allowing love its space to simply be.
We lean into this wordless communion,
where presence speaks more than any sound.
Each silence becomes a familiar step,
a path we walk without fear or demand.
Together we stand on this bridge of calm,
a quiet promise, steadfast and warm.

In the Space We Share

In the space where words do not intrude,
we find ourselves wrapped in quiet promise.
Our love doesn't need constant reminder—
its depth is known in the calm between us.
Years add strength to this silent foundation,
binding us with gentle assurance,
a knowing that grows deeper, unsaid yet felt,
where trust is kept in the space we share.
We have built this bridge with patient silence,
each quiet moment a brick in its span.
This vow unspoken, yet never in doubt,
holds us steady through all life's tempests.
With each passing day, this silence endures,
a bridge we walk that feels calm and sure.

A Quiet Understanding

Our understanding lies beyond words,
a bridge we built without the need to speak.
It grows stronger with each quiet moment,
a silent promise woven by time.
This bond is a place we trust deeply,
a comfort we know without saying so.
Our love holds its shape in every pause,
a steady calm that silence alone knows.
When words are not enough, we return here,
finding peace in the space we have crafted,
a sanctuary that we carry with us,
built on years of quiet assurance.
In silence, our vows hold and remain true,
a quiet bridge between me and you.

First Light

In the pale glow of dawn, words feel distant,
replaced by the warmth of shared stillness.
Your glance holds a promise, soft and sure,
a vow bound in morning's gentle light.
Each silent look is a quiet assurance,
a pledge we make without speaking,
held in the calm before the world wakes,
when only we exist in this fragile peace.
In these first moments, nothing needs saying—
we find each other without sound or rush,
making promises with only our breath.

Waking in Silence

The day begins in soft, unhurried steps,
and we meet in glances, wrapped in calm.
No words pass between us, yet it's enough,
this silent promise that the morning holds.
Our eyes meet, and in that quiet exchange,
a vow is made to carry each other gently,
to walk through whatever the day may bring,
grounded in the peace of this morning pause.
These promises linger beyond dawn's light,
unspoken yet steady as a heartbeat,
woven into each morning we share.

Held by the Quiet

In the early light, I find you there,
a familiar shape wrapped in gentle calm.
No sound breaks the morning's embrace,
only a glance that holds me close.
This silence is a promise in itself,
an understanding bound in trust and ease.
In these first moments, we need no words—
just the quiet vow that morning gifts us.
With each dawn, this bond renews itself,
a promise held by the quiet of daybreak,
sealed in the warmth of shared stillness.

Soft Beginnings

Morning comes slow, gentle as a breath,
and in this hush, I feel your silent vow.
It's not in words, but in the look we share,
a promise woven by the touch of dawn.
Your glance speaks softly, a vow without sound,
carried in the warmth of this quiet start.
In these moments, we hold something deeper,
an unspoken trust to face the day as one.
Each dawn is a chance to renew this bond,
to find ourselves in the peace of morning,
wrapped in promises only silence knows.

Whispers of Daybreak

The world holds its breath as morning unfolds,
and in that pause, I feel the promise grow—
a silent vow resting in your gaze,
an oath made real by morning's gentle touch.
No words fill the space, yet it's enough,
this quiet understanding we share.
We find each other anew each dawn,
bound by the calm that the light unveils.
This is a promise of presence, of peace,
held softly in the morning's first embrace,
a vow to keep through each waking day.

Silent Oaths

In the pale glow before the sun arrives,
we make our promises without words,
meeting in glances, soft and steady,
a quiet oath to greet the day together.
Each look holds a trust, simple and true,
a vow to be held close as morning breaks.
The silence between us speaks of care,
of the gentle faith we find in day's first light.
Every morning, this promise renews,
a silent oath shared with dawn's arrival,
carried in the peace of early hours.

A Language All Our Own

In a crowded room, you catch my eye,
and a smile passes like a secret note,
telling me everything without a word—
a language only we know, soft and true.
With that look, you say all there is to say,
and I respond with a quiet grin,
a knowing that needs no explanation,
just the trust we hold in each other's gaze.
These smiles carry more than any words—
a promise, a memory, a spark of joy,
a silent exchange only we understand.

Hidden in Plain Sight

A smile shared across the room,
an entire conversation in one glance—
the way your eyes meet mine and soften,
a private moment no one else can see.
We laugh without sound, share thoughts unspoken,
in a look that bridges time and space.
It's enough to feel that gentle spark,
a small exchange that carries so much.
Our smiles tell stories only we know,
wrapped in memories and whispered dreams,
hidden in plain sight, but ours alone.

Silent Conversations

Your smile says everything—
more than words could ever hope to hold.
In that curve, I find the answer,
a warmth that fills the space between.
Without a sound, we share a moment,
a whole conversation held in one look,
speaking in quiet lines and glances,
a private language all our own.
What we share is hidden from the world,
a quiet joy exchanged in secret smiles,
a conversation known only to us.

A Glance Across the Room

In the smallest grin, a universe unfolds—
a whole story told in one quiet look.
It's the way you smile when you see me,
a glance that feels like coming home.
We don't need words to say what's there,
to know the thoughts we share, unspoken.
A smile, a raised brow, a soft laugh—
we tell it all in those brief exchanges.
Our eyes meet, and something timeless lingers,
a spark of recognition, of secret knowing,
held safe within a simple smile.

Of Laughs and Glances

In the curve of your smile, I find my place,
a wordless world only we inhabit,
where each grin holds a thousand meanings,
conversations carried in knowing glances.
You look at me, and something clicks,
an understanding deep as any vow.
We share a laugh without a sound,
a gentle joke only we would know.
This is our quiet, tender language—
spoken in smiles and echoed in hearts,
an endless dialogue we never voice.

Unseen by the World

Our smiles are notes in a silent song,
a melody played in glances and grins,
hidden from those who don't understand
the love that speaks in quiet exchanges.
With just one look, you tell me enough,
and I answer in a smile of my own.
No words are needed, just that spark,
a connection strong and silent between us.
We smile, and the world falls away,
leaving only this shared, secret place,
a conversation written without words.

Family & Bonds

Echoes of Their Hands

In the quiet gestures we carry forward,
the way our hands move through daily tasks,
there is a legacy, silent but steady,
a promise held in each familiar motion.
They did not need to say what mattered;
they showed it, in how they faced each day,
in the resilience of calloused fingers,
in the grace that marked their simplest acts.
Through unspoken vows, we know their strength,
the quiet endurance that endures in us.
Their voices linger in the spaces between,
a reminder to hold fast, to move with care.
We walk paths they forged without a word,
inheriting promises woven into our bones,
a legacy passed down through gentle silence.

Bound by Their Quiet Resolve

We carry their silence like a steady weight,
a strength that asks no praise, no notice.
It's in the way we stand firm in storms,
in the way we hold our ground, unspeaking.
Their lessons are etched into our gestures,
wisdom shared without the need for words.
They left no grand speeches, no loud calls,
just a knowing we keep close, in stillness.
We inherit their resolve in quiet ways,
a vow to honour what they held dear,
to be guardians of their unspoken truths,
the values they lived, unsung but enduring.
This silence becomes our foundation,
an inheritance that shapes us from within,
binding us to a legacy we silently keep.

In the Shadows of Their Footsteps

Their steps left marks that we cannot see,
but feel beneath each choice, each path.
They spoke not of burdens, only carried them,
teaching us strength without saying how.
Their lives are woven through our own,
a pattern held in quiet reverence.
In their silence, we find our guidance,
a compass we hold, though unseen.
What they gave us was never loud,
but strong and rooted, a steady guide.
We walk paths lined with their wisdom,
each step a quiet promise to honour them.
We inherit their patience, their quiet faith,
passed down in gestures, glances, nods,
a silent legacy that steers us forward.

The Unheard Lessons

What they taught us was never spoken,
yet we feel it in the marrow of our bones—
a knowing that comes without words,
a promise to hold what they cherished.
Their lives were marked by unspoken vows,
by duties carried without complaint.
They did not tell us to be strong,
they showed us in each silent act of care.
This is the legacy they left behind,
a quiet strength that does not waver.
In every choice we make, we honour them,
our lives shaped by their silent guidance.
The weight of their silence stays with us,
not as a burden, but as a gift,
an inheritance of strength beyond words.

Between Generations

They left no written promises,
no words to bind us to their dreams.
Instead, their silence holds us close,
a bond that endures beyond language.
We know their hopes in the way we live,
in the patience we carry, unspoken.
Their values hum beneath each breath,
whispering truths we may never name.
Through every quiet act, we remember them,
the ones who lived without loud vows,
who taught us in stillness and care,
their legacy growing, unseen, within.
What they gave lives on in silence,
a heritage we keep without effort,
their dreams folded gently into our own.

The Weight of Their Silence

We are bound by what they did not say,
the silent promises kept close to heart.
They spoke not of legacy, yet left it,
an inheritance held in acts, not words.
In each gentle touch, each steady look,
they passed on more than they could know.
We live with their quiet faith in us,
a trust that we would carry them forward.
There is no need to speak of duty,
no words required for this bond we share.
Their silence holds all we need to know,
a steady hand we feel guiding us.
Through us, their silent vows remain,
a quiet strength that will not fade,
an unspoken legacy we carry still.

Unseen Watchers

They move softly, unseen, in spaces we can't sense,
guardians who need no praise, no acknowledgment,
only the quiet peace of knowing we are safe.
They hold a thousand promises in their steady hands.
In the shadow of their love, we find our footing,
their silent vow a shield we never need to ask for.
Each day, they keep us steady, anchoring us,
ensuring we grow strong, grounded in their care.
We walk forward, unaware of the watchful eyes,
yet feeling the warmth, the protection they offer,
a shelter built on their unspoken promise.
They remain near, close enough to hold if we stumble.
Without words, they guide us through life's unknowns,
their presence like a shadow, patient and true,
a guardian bound by quiet, enduring love.

Invisible Shields

In the quiet hours, they are awake,
whispering silent promises into our dreams,
vows of protection woven in their gaze,
watching over us as we rest, unaware.
Their strength lies hidden, quiet and calm,
a shelter built of invisible walls.
They promise to stand, to carry, to hold,
without words, only with steady resolve.
Their love moves like a shadow at our side,
never asking for thanks, never faltering,
a silent pledge that keeps us anchored, safe.
We walk through life, wrapped in their silent care.
Even when far, we feel their presence close,
guardians bound by vows they never spoke aloud,
a love so constant it becomes our air.

Promises in the Quiet

There's a promise in the way they look at us,
a quiet assurance, a gentle resolve,
a vow they make in every touch, every glance,
to guide, protect, and never let us fall.
They walk beside us, close enough to catch,
yet giving space to let our wings unfold.
They hold their hopes, dreams, and fears for us,
tucked safely in the silence of their hearts.
We don't hear their vows, but we feel them all the same,
a steady presence that asks for nothing in return.
Their love is a promise, patient and deep,
binding them to us, without need for words.
They are guardians, shadows moving with us,
holding us safe in their silent devotion,
their love our shelter, fierce and unseen.

A Silent Pledge

In their footsteps, we find our path,
their silent promise woven through each step.
They do not speak of the burdens they carry,
yet we feel their strength in every glance.
They give without end, their love unasked,
a guardian's shadow in our brightest light.
Through their quiet vow, we learn resilience,
knowing they will catch us if we fall.
Their promises are soft, like whispered breaths,
a steady presence that we come to trust.
They promise to stand, to guide, to hold,
without demand, just a constant, silent care.
Their love is a promise that shields us still,
a guardian's shadow, constant and calm,
the silent pledge that lets us fly.

A Promise Kept in Shadows

They stand behind, just out of sight,
close enough to catch if we should stumble,
yet far enough to let us find our way.
Their love is a promise we never hear aloud.
In every moment, they keep their silent oath,
a vow to protect, to guide us through unknowns.
They give their dreams to see ours bloom,
their strength a quiet gift, unseen but true.
We may not always see them watching close,
but their shadow moves with each step we take,
an unspoken promise to shelter and support.
Through their care, we learn the courage to grow.
They guard us gently, bound by silent love,
holding their promises deep, just for us,
a guardian's shadow, patient and proud.

Bound by Love, Silent and Strong

Their hands guide us, though we may not see,
moving quietly, a promise woven in love.
They do not speak of what they would give,
their sacrifices kept close, silent, sure.
They vow to protect without need for thanks,
a guardian's shadow that stays with us, unseen.
In their silent watch, we find our courage,
knowing they will always stand, just nearby.
Their love remains steady, a promise unvoiced,
a bond that holds us, even from afar.
They trust us to grow, to rise, to find our way,
yet their silent promise is to always be there.
Their strength, their love, is a shadow we carry,
a quiet vow that never fades away,
a promise, silent yet fierce and unwavering.

A Pact Beyond Words

Between us lies a quiet understanding,
a promise not made with words but with time.
We've learned to carry each other's burdens,
to share what feels too heavy alone.
In moments of joy, we are each other's first call,
in moments of sorrow, each other's safe haven.
We do not need to ask for help,
it is simply there, in looks and gestures.
We move together through life's storms,
an unbreakable line against the world.
What weighs on one, the other lifts,
what one fears, the other guards.
Bound by something deeper than language,
we stand side by side, silent and strong,
carrying each other, no matter the weight.

Beneath the Surface

We speak in glances, in quiet nods,
a language known only to us,
where burdens are passed in silence,
and strength is lent without request.
We share the weight that life lays down,
never counting, never keeping score.
What one of us cannot bear alone,
the other takes, without a second thought.
In our bond lies a silent pledge,
a pact to stand, come what may.
Through every trial, we find our way,
with the promise of a steady shoulder.
We are more than just siblings;
we are each other's safe place,
holding the weight together, always.

Unseen Vows

We didn't need to say it out loud—
the vow was there in every fight,
every laugh, every shared secret.
A quiet promise formed over years.
Life's burdens come, and without words,
we take turns holding what needs held.
When I falter, you are there,
a steady hand, a grounding force.
Together, we face what life demands,
a silent agreement in place.
We do not falter, we do not break;
we stand strong, with shoulders aligned.
Through laughter, through pain, we hold fast,
each other's quiet refuge, safe and true,
bound by a vow we never had to speak.

An Unbreakable Thread

In the spaces where words fall short,
our bond fills the silence with strength.
We carry what we cannot speak of,
a shared weight neither of us denies.
Through every burden, we are there,
side by side, as steady as stone.
What feels too much alone is lighter,
split between us, carried in turns.
Our lives wind together, woven tight,
each thread an unspoken promise kept.
We are bound by loyalty and love,
by an oath we never had to make.
In this bond, we find our courage,
in this bond, we find our peace.
Together, we share the weight of life,
each other's steadfast, silent ally.

Through Every Storm

There is strength in knowing we stand as one,
a quiet trust that never wavers.
No burden feels too heavy to bear
when we carry it side by side.
In moments of laughter, in times of grief,
we find each other without asking.
This silent promise binds us close,
an understanding deep and pure.
What weighs on one, both shoulders share,
a bond that life's storms cannot break.
With you, I find the courage to face
whatever comes, no matter the cost.
We are guardians for one another,
lifting each other through darkest days,
an unspoken vow to always be there.

Anchored by Love

Between us lies a promise unspoken,
an oath that holds us steady and true.
We do not need to say the words aloud—
we simply know we will stand by each other.
Through days of sunlight, nights of rain,
we share the weight of life's demands.
What feels too heavy to hold alone
becomes lighter when carried together.
You are my anchor, my strength, my home,
a presence constant as the stars.
We lift each other in silent grace,
each burden split, each sorrow shared.
Bound by something fierce and steadfast,
we walk through life as more than friends.
We are each other's unbreakable shield,
promising, always, to shoulder the load.

A Language Beyond Words

In the space where words fall short,
our bond lives, quiet yet unbreakable,
a language woven through years of knowing,
a comfort that does not ask or need.
There is no need to explain or ask—
our glances hold all that words would lose.
Each shared silence carries a gentle strength,
an understanding steady and sure.
In laughter, in grief, in moments of calm,
we find each other without needing sound.
These threads between us hold tight and true,
binding us close with invisible ties.
Through every storm, each joy, every calm,
this unspoken connection endures,
a quiet promise, constant as breath,
an unbroken thread woven through our lives.

Held in Silence

We sit together, words unneeded,
finding peace in each other's presence.
Our bond does not demand conversation;
it is simply there, woven into us.
A quiet look says what we both know,
a nod that holds years of shared memory.
We walk through life anchored in silence,
our unbroken thread tying us close.
There is comfort in knowing you are near,
in the stillness that we do not fill,
for silence speaks more than words could hold,
and presence alone is its own promise.
These threads between us, unseen, unworn,
are bound by trust and quiet love,
a family bond unspoken, yet strong,
holding us close with no need for sound.

Threads of Understanding

Between us lies a thread unseen,
a connection held without demand,
a quiet bond that does not waver,
formed through years of shared life and love.
We do not need to speak of loyalty,
for it's stitched into each memory.
In moments of laughter, of shared tears,
we find strength in the silence between.
A look, a smile, a gentle nod—
these speak louder than words could bear.
Our lives are bound by this silent thread,
woven through time and all we've shared.
This bond is unbroken, steady, true,
a presence that's felt, not needing words,
our quiet understanding, deep and calm,
an unspoken promise that we hold close.

Silent Assurance

In the quiet moments, words fall away,
and all that's left is presence, calm and sure.
A hand held, a shoulder close by,
no need to say more than the nearness allows.
We speak in breaths, in the space we share,
in knowing that simply being here is enough.
This language doesn't rely on words,
but on the steady promise of staying.
You are there, and that's all I need,
a quiet comfort that does not falter,
a silent strength that fills the room,
a warmth that speaks louder than sound.
In your presence, I find my peace,
in knowing I'm never truly alone.

The Gift of Being Here

Your presence holds a language all its own,
a gentle promise that words can't match.
You sit with me, unhurried, calm,
and I know I'm held without needing to ask.
In stillness, you say what I need to hear,
without speaking, yet fully understood.
Your being here is a vow unbroken,
a reminder that I am not alone.
Sometimes love is simply staying close,
a quiet presence that asks nothing back,
a gift that reassures with just a look,
a warmth that only silence holds.
In your steady presence, I find my rest,
a promise kept by simply being here.

When Words Are Not Enough

Sometimes words are too fragile, too small,
to carry the weight of what we need.
Instead, you are here, a steady calm,
and I know, in your quiet, I am seen.
Your presence is a language deep and true,
a silent vow that does not need sound.
We sit in stillness, without demands,
letting this moment be all it is.
You say everything with just your gaze,
your being here more than enough.
In the quiet, I find a gentle strength,
a promise bound in patient calm.
Here, in your silence, I feel complete,
knowing your presence is all I need.

Holding and Releasing

You gave me roots, deep and steady,
a foundation I could call my own.
In your arms, I found safety, shelter,
a place to grow, to know I belonged.
But as I grew, you quietly stepped back,
giving me wings in ways I didn't see.
An unspoken agreement: to protect, to guide,
yet to let me find the sky on my own.
I could feel your silent promise in each step,
the gentle push forward, the steady hand.
You taught me how to stand on my own
and whispered I would know when to fly.
Now I carry your strength wherever I go,
rooted in love, lifted by your trust,
a bond of roots and wings that holds me still.

The Gift of Flight

Your hands held me close, tender and sure,
as you built my world with care and patience.
Through the years, you planted seeds of strength,
watching them grow, never asking for thanks.
You gave me all I needed to grow,
the roots of love, the soil of kindness,
yet you knew, always, that I would leave,
that someday I'd need the gift of flight.
Without words, you let me find my way,
a silent promise to be there, always.
You are the ground beneath my steps,
the wind that lifts me when I falter.
Roots and wings, given without a sound,
a balance of holding on and letting go,
a quiet agreement woven into love.

A Balance of Love

In the quiet moments, you taught me well,
not through words but by the way you loved—
a steady hand to guide, an open door,
roots to ground me, wings to help me soar.
I felt your protection, soft but strong,
the trust that let me wander, yet return.
You gave me the freedom to be my own,
knowing one day I'd take to the sky.
The unspoken promise between us held firm—
to protect as long as I needed a home,
to release when I was ready to fly,
a love that knows both holding and letting go.
You gave me roots deep as the earth,
and wings light as the open air,
a legacy of trust to carry me on.

Friendship & Connection

Invisible Threads

Miles stretch between us, but we remain,
bound by threads that distance cannot break.
We don't need to speak of our friendship—
it exists in the quiet, in spaces we hold.
Through years and miles, we stay connected,
a promise unspoken yet always felt.
Your voice echoes in my thoughts, gentle,
whispering reminders of all we've shared.
We do not need to say we'll be there;
the distance only strengthens the knowing.
We are woven together by memory,
by laughter and tears that need no words.
Across time zones, our bond holds fast,
a friendship held in invisible threads,
unbreakable, steady, no matter the miles.

A Silent Understanding

In each message, each delayed response,
our friendship flows, unshaken by space.
We don't need reminders or frequent calls—
just the trust that exists in silence.
You are here, though you're far away,
a constant presence felt deep within.
Our unspoken promise rests between us,
a quiet vow to stand by, no matter what.
We hold each other close in spirit,
even when time and distance intervene.
This bond is built on quiet loyalty,
a trust that doesn't ask for proof.
We know, without saying, we will remain,
friends across miles, rooted in care,
our voices carried by whispers of love.

Echoes in the Silence

Across oceans, in cities unknown to me,
you live, yet it feels as though you're near.
There is no need for daily words;
our friendship lies in the spaces between.
We carry each other in unspoken ways,
in memories that feel like home.
You are present in each quiet thought,
a companion woven into my days.
Distance changes nothing we share—
I feel you here, steady as breath.
We are bound by whispers, unseen, unfading,
a promise that lives beyond sight or sound.
We are close in ways that miles can't touch,
a friendship that time and space cannot alter,
held in the silence that binds us true.

Anchored in Memory

Our friendship rests on shared memory,
moments held in the warmth of recall.
We may not be able to meet as before,
yet you're here in ways that matter more.
The miles fade in laughter remembered,
in knowing glances, in thoughts exchanged.
We have an understanding beyond words,
an anchor that keeps us steady, always.
Our unspoken promise spans the miles,
an invisible thread of trust and care.
I feel your presence as surely as my own,
a friend woven into the fabric of me.
We remain anchored, despite the distance,
an unbreakable bond stretched across time,
held in the silent promise of true friends.

A Quiet Loyalty

In the silence between our conversations,
a promise waits, patient and true.
Though distance separates, it can't erase
the steady vow of our friendship's grace.
We don't speak of the miles that divide;
our loyalty doesn't waver or dim.
It rests in the moments we shared before,
in memories held close, unforgotten.
We trust in a bond beyond sight and sound,
a friendship that doesn't demand proof.
Though far, you are as near as a heartbeat,
a silent presence that fills my days.
We are bound by whispers across the miles,
a quiet pledge that lives in each thought,
a promise that distance cannot undo.

Silent Strength

When storms rage and I feel unmoored,
you're there, solid as a lighthouse.
No words are needed, no grand gestures,
just your quiet presence beside me.
You are the anchor in my restless sea,
a calm reminder that I am not alone.
With you, I find my footing again,
steady and sure, even in the dark.
Your silence speaks louder than words,
a friendship built on quiet strength,
an anchor holding me through the storm.

A Steady Hand

In times of trouble, you appear,
a steady hand without a single sound.
You don't rush to fill the silence,
but offer space for me to breathe.
With you, I don't need explanations;
you know, without needing to ask.
Your presence brings a quiet calm,
a gentle anchor when I am adrift.
Together we sit in unspoken peace,
a friendship rooted deep and strong,
an anchor I hold to when waves rise.

Unspoken Comfort

In my darkest hours, you are there,
not to fix, but simply to be.
Your silent support holds me steady,
an anchor unseen yet deeply felt.
I find comfort in your quiet gaze,
in the way you sit, calm and near.
No words are needed to feel your care,
your presence speaks what you don't say.
In your stillness, I find my strength,
a grounding force through every storm,
an anchor waiting, constant and true.

When Words Fall Short

You arrive when words feel useless,
when comfort can't be spoken aloud.
In your silence, I feel understood,
a friend who knows what cannot be said.
You stand beside me, steady and calm,
holding space for me to gather strength.
Your presence is my quiet anchor,
a reminder that I don't stand alone.
Together we weather the hardest storms,
bound by trust that needs no words,
an anchor resting deep in shared silence.

A Quiet Presence

You don't need to offer advice or fix,
just being here is all I need.
In your quiet presence, I find peace,
an anchor holding strong and steady.
With you, there's no need to explain;
you know my storms without asking why.
Your silent support is unbreakable,
a bond that weathers every tide.
In your calm, I feel my own strength rise,
a friendship held without a single word,
an anchor I return to, time and again.

The Quiet Applause

I see your hard work pay off,
the dreams you've nurtured finally in bloom.
You stand, glowing with quiet pride,
and I feel a joy that words can't touch.
I cheer silently, a friend in the wings,
watching you shine, strong and true.
My pride for you doesn't need to be loud;
it's steady, deep, felt in every glance.
In your triumph, I see all the hours,
the moments of doubt you pushed through,
and I celebrate, knowing how far you've come,
how each step has led you here.
This quiet pride is its own applause,
a friendship woven in joy for you,
a silent cheer that rings clear and true.

Witness to Your Journey

I stand back, watching you soar,
my heart filled with pride, unspoken yet real.
It's a quiet happiness, a gentle glow,
a joy shared without needing words.
I saw the work, the long nights,
the resilience you carried like a flame.
Now you stand, triumphant, unwavering,
and I am there, quietly cheering you on.
Your success is a testament to strength,
and I feel honoured to bear witness.
This is our shared victory, in a way,
a triumph I celebrate as if my own.
For in your joy, I find my own,
a silent cheer that knows no bounds,
a friendship woven through pride and grace.

In the Background, Proud

Your achievements shine, bold and true,
and in the background, I quietly smile.
I don't need to say how proud I am,
you feel it in the way I look your way.
I celebrate each step you've taken,
knowing the journey you've endured.
It's a pride that fills my heart softly,
an unspoken joy that needs no sound.
When you reach a milestone, I feel it,
as if your victory lifts us both.
This quiet pride is my way of saying,
I see you, I celebrate you, I am here.
Our friendship holds space for this joy,
a bond where pride lives, loud or soft,
a silent cheer that stands beside you.

The Joy of Watching You Rise

You've reached heights I always knew you would,
and in the silence, I feel my heart lift.
There's no need to shout my pride aloud;
it's a quiet joy that fills the air.
I see the victories that you now claim,
and each one brings a subtle cheer.
You may not hear it, but it's there,
a presence warm as a gentle embrace.
Every achievement, every goal met,
feels like a triumph shared between us.
I hold this pride close, quietly thrilled,
knowing your journey was worth each step.
I am here, a friend in quiet awe,
celebrating you with silent cheers,
a happiness shared in the softest way.

A Pride Unsaid

In your success, I find my own joy,
a quiet pride that fills each glance.
I don't need to say how proud I am—
it's there in the way I stand by you.
This is your moment, and I honour it,
celebrating in a silence warm and true.
I watched you rise, step by step,
and now, seeing you shine, my heart lifts.
Each achievement is a silent cheer,
a testament to all you've overcome.
Your victory feels like a shared breath,
a joy I carry with quiet pride.
We don't need words to feel this bond;
it's woven in every triumph we hold,
a friendship that lifts in silent applause.

The Guardians of Our Past

We are each other's memory keepers,
holding moments the world may forget.
In laughter and sorrow, we hold them close,
preserving the pieces that make us whole.
We remember the nights spent talking,
the quiet tears and whispered dreams,
the laughter that lingered long after,
each memory a promise we silently keep.
These memories are treasures we guard,
pieces of us that no one else knows.
Through time, they grow softer, warmer,
but they never lose their weight or worth.
As long as we hold them, they live on,
reminders of who we were, who we are,
a silent vow to never let them fade.

Sacred Moments Shared

With you, memories feel like sacred ground,
moments we protect with gentle hands.
We carry each other's stories forward,
each one a vow, a quiet promise.
You remember things I may forget,
a mirror reflecting pieces of me,
and I hold fragments of you as well,
pieces woven into who we've become.
In our friendship, we preserve the past,
small moments others might let slip.
They're safe here, held like precious stones,
a collection only we understand.
Together, we keep the stories alive,
keepers of laughter, love, and light,
guardians of memories we never outgrow.

The Weight of What We Share

We hold each other's memories in trust,
guarding them as sacred promises,
moments only we know the weight of,
shared years stitched into our souls.
You remember my first heartbreak,
the dreams I whispered in the dark.
I remember your laugh in quiet spaces,
the way you shone in unexpected light.
These memories are held, unspoken vows,
a promise to carry the past with care.
We share a history no one else can see,
built on silent glances and gentle nods.
Through years, through distance, we remain,
keepers of each other's lives,
guarding memories like precious secrets.

Bound by Memory

We walk through life as memory keepers,
holding sacred the moments we shared.
You hold pieces of me that I've lost,
and I carry memories of you like heirlooms.
In our friendship, the past is safe,
preserved in the warmth of quiet trust.
We keep each other's joys and sorrows,
never letting them drift away.
These memories are promises we don't forget,
sacred vows held close to heart.
They're stories woven into us both,
a silent bond that strengthens with time.
No matter where life may take us next,
we are bound by what we've kept alive,
keepers of a shared, cherished past.

The Strength of Quiet Presence

You sit beside me, no words exchanged,
offering comfort I can feel in silence.
There's a strength in knowing I don't need to explain,
that your presence alone is my safe place.
In moments when words fall short or fail,
you become a quiet anchor in the storm.
I lean on you, feeling understood,
without having to say a single thing.
There's a beauty in a friend who listens deeply,
even when no sounds are made, no confessions shared.
Your shoulder is a place I can lean into,
knowing my burden is somehow lighter.
This is a comfort that words cannot hold,
a bond woven from the gentle act of staying,
a quiet trust that says, "I am here for you."

A Silent Kind of Strength

There are days when words feel heavy,
too tangled to speak, too complex to share.
In those moments, you are simply there,
your presence a quiet strength I can hold.
You don't ask for answers I can't give,
or search for meanings I'm not ready to find.
Instead, you stay with a calm, gentle grace,
a support that never pressures or pries.
I find peace in this silence we share,
in knowing you understand without knowing why.
Your shoulder is a resting place I trust,
a shelter that requires nothing in return.
Through silence, you show me care that's deep,
a friendship that listens beyond words,
a space where I can be, simply as I am.

In the Quiet of Friendship

In the stillness, I feel your steady presence,
a warmth that fills the silence without force.
You sit with me in my quiet grief,
no need for words to soothe or explain.
It's enough to know you're by my side,
offering comfort through simple being.
This quiet companionship speaks of trust,
a bond that holds more than language could.
You offer a shoulder without asking why,
a silent promise to share what I carry.
With you, I am allowed to just exist,
to find peace in not having to explain.
This is friendship in its truest form,
a space of gentle understanding and care,
a quiet knowing that I am not alone.

Unspoken Comfort

There are things I cannot put into words,
thoughts too tangled to make sense aloud.
Yet in your company, I find a peace,
a shoulder I can lean on without reason.
You sit with me, no answers required,
offering presence as a balm, a trust.
Your silence is a language all its own,
a reassurance that I am safe here.
With you, there's no need to explain my heart,
no expectation to make sense of my mind.
I feel your quiet support, patient and calm,
a friendship built on simply being near.
This silent comfort speaks of strength,
a bond woven in moments without sound,
an unspoken understanding that I am seen.

Self-Reflection & Growth

Reflections of Resolve

In the stillness, I see my own gaze,
a quiet promise resting in my eyes.
There are vows I've made, softly spoken,
echoes that linger, shaping my path.
Each morning, I meet myself anew,
reminded of the strength I carry.
These promises hum beneath the surface,
a steady rhythm, a silent guide.
They tell me to rise, to try again,
even when the road feels steep.
They remind me of resilience, patience,
the quiet courage I've vowed to keep.
In the mirror, I find these echoes strong,
promises that live deep within,
binding me to the person I am becoming.

Whispers of Self-Trust

When I look into my own reflection,
I see promises not meant for words,
commitments made in the quiet hours,
vows I hold close, unseen but fierce.
They are small oaths of kindness, of strength,
a gentle trust I extend to myself.
They are the choices I make each day,
the resolve to move forward, to keep growing.
In my reflection, I find the weight
of these silent promises I carry.
They are the foundation beneath my feet,
a reminder of who I strive to be.
With each glance, I renew them again,
those whispered vows to honour my path,
to be true to the person I'm becoming.

Promises in Silence

I meet my own eyes in the mirror's gaze,
and in that quiet, a promise stirs.
No words needed, just a knowing resolve,
an echo of vows made to myself.
There are things I've promised to hold close—
strength in times of doubt, calm in storms,
a commitment to kindness, to resilience,
to honour the journey I'm called to walk.
These promises shape my steps each day,
a silent compass, guiding my way.
They remind me to stand, to stay true,
to embrace the person I am and will be.
In the mirror, these echoes live on,
each one a quiet pillar of strength,
a promise that binds me to my own truth.

Reflections Unspoken

In the still reflection, I see a vow,
a promise made without need for sound.
It's a commitment to become, to rise,
to honour the self I am meant to be.
These silent promises hold me steady,
a whispered guide through life's unknowns.
They tell me to trust, to seek, to grow,
to be both soft and unbreakable.
They live in each choice, each quiet thought,
in the moments when I am alone.
They are the promises I keep for myself,
the strength I build, unspoken yet true.
In my reflection, I see them shine—
a quiet pledge to hold, to heal, to grow,
to become the echo I see looking back.

The Promise of Morning

Each day, a silent vow is made,
a promise that whispers in the dawn—
to rise, to greet whatever comes,
to stand despite the weight of yesterday.
It isn't a loud, triumphant oath,
but a quiet resolve within the soul.
No matter how the night has lingered,
the morning brings a steady chance to begin.
I wake with this vow held close,
an anchor to pull me through each hour.
Some days, it feels as light as breath,
on others, as heavy as the world itself.
But still, I rise, renewed and grounded,
bound to this promise to carry on,
to find strength in simply standing again.

Unseen Strength

In the early light, I feel the weight,
but also the promise I made long ago—
a quiet vow to keep going, to rise,
to face the dawn, no matter the night.
It's a choice repeated with each breath,
a decision not to yield to shadows.
Some days, it's a struggle, a climb,
yet I find in myself this steady resolve.
I've promised myself to keep moving,
to let resilience be my daily prayer.
I rise because there's power in trying,
in finding courage within each step.
This vow doesn't ask for grand gestures,
just the strength to stand and try anew,
a promise to meet each day, whatever it brings.

A Quiet Promise

There is a vow I hold each dawn,
a quiet promise that stirs as I wake—
to rise, no matter the weight I carry,
to face the light, no matter the dark.
It's not a vow spoken aloud,
but one that lives deep in my chest.
Some days, it feels as simple as breath,
and others, a mountain I climb alone.
Yet still, I stand, renewed in resolve,
lifting myself with each new day.
This commitment holds me, steady and true,
a promise of strength, of silent grace.
I rise because there is beauty in trying,
in honouring the self that chooses to stand,
in the quiet vow to always rise again.

A Quiet Kindness

Today, I promise to ease my tone,
to soften the words I speak to myself.
I'll hold my flaws with gentle hands,
letting kindness fill the gaps within.
I am learning to forgive, to release,
to let go of sharp edges, piece by piece.
No longer bound by harsh critique,
I'll welcome warmth where judgment was.
Each day, I renew this silent vow—
to be patient, to be tender, to be whole,
to soften into a friend I'd keep close.

Learning to Let Go

I'm teaching myself the art of grace,
to let go of the need for perfection.
To soften the edges I've long held tight,
and breathe more room into who I am.
Each day, I give myself a little more,
a chance to be less than polished, fine.
In moments of doubt, I pause, forgive,
finding beauty in letting mistakes be.
This is the quiet promise I make—
to carry myself gently, without rush,
to honour the journey, however flawed.

Gentle Reminders

There are whispers I offer myself,
small reminders to slow, to be kind.
I promise to meet each fault with grace,
to soften the edges I once made sharp.
Today, I choose to be a bit gentler,
to greet my own heart with open arms.
In learning to love each imperfect part,
I find the strength I was seeking all along.
This is the vow I renew each day—
to see myself through a softer lens,
to cherish who I am, just as I am.

Becoming My Own Friend

I am learning to soften the way I see,
to become my own friend in quiet ways.
Instead of demands, I offer care,
a promise to hold myself with warmth.
Each fault, each flaw, I welcome near,
a gentle acceptance replacing critique.
I make room for mistakes without shame,
allowing myself to simply be.
This is the kindness I owe myself,
a vow to honour my own soft heart,
to meet my reflection with open grace.

The Room to Become

I'm learning to hold space for myself,
to give room for growth that can't be rushed.
In stillness, I find the beginnings of peace,
a quiet promise to nurture what's within.
There's no need to rush this healing journey,
no hurry to be perfect or whole at once.
I am here, allowing myself to unfold,
each small step a testament to patience.
In this space, I honour my own becoming,
letting go of timelines, of pressures,
and choosing instead to breathe, to pause,
to listen to the rhythms of my heart.
I am a work in progress, and that is enough,
a soul expanding in soft, steady ways,
holding space to grow, to heal, to be free.

A Gentle Sanctuary

I create a sanctuary within,
a space untouched by doubt or fear,
where I am allowed to grow slowly,
where my healing has room to breathe.
This is a place for self-compassion,
for forgiving mistakes I've yet to release,
a space that honours all I am becoming,
and all the wounds I am ready to soothe.
I hold space for my own journey forward,
for dreams yet fragile, for steps unsteady,
giving myself the grace to learn,
to stumble, to rise, and try again.
In this quiet haven, I let myself be,
free from expectation, from any rush,
a place to heal, to change, to belong to myself.

The Strength Beneath Silence

There is a courage not often seen,
a strength that lives in silent resolve.
To rise each day, bearing unseen burdens,
without a word, without a need for show.
This is the unvoiced bravery we hold,
the silent will to keep moving forward.
It's in each quiet step we take alone,
a journey made with courage unshared.
Though no one sees the weight we carry,
we know the resilience it demands.
In the stillness, we find our own strength,
the power to keep walking through storms.
It is a courage that needs no applause,
a strength unspoken but deeply true,
a quiet heroism we honour ourselves.

Walking Unseen Paths

Each day, we shoulder what others can't see,
silent struggles tucked deep within.
There is bravery in unshared battles,
a quiet resilience born in the dark.
We walk paths no one else may notice,
finding strength in our own steady steps.
There's a power in moving through pain alone,
in knowing our own courage without praise.
These are the moments we grow within,
becoming stronger without the need for show.
No witness is needed to see this fight—
we carry it, fierce and without sound.
In each unvoiced stride, we prove our strength,
honouring a courage no words could hold,
an inner victory we keep to ourselves.

The Quiet Resolve

Beneath the surface, strength remains unseen,
a will to endure when no one knows.
We rise without telling of the battles fought,
moving forward through silent storms.
There's bravery in holding our own pain,
a quiet power that asks for no praise.
We gather courage in each private breath,
in each moment we choose to carry on.
This is the resilience of those who stay,
who fight alone yet refuse to yield.
The world may not see our steady resolve,
but we know the depth of our own quiet might.
In silence, we honour the courage we hold,
a strength beyond words, resilient and real,
the unvoiced courage to simply keep going.

Nature & the Universe

Under the Quiet Moon

Beneath the night sky, beneath the stars,
I make silent promises no one hears.
The moon listens to my whispered hopes,
a witness to vows held close to heart.
I stand alone, bathed in gentle light,
finding courage in the vast, still dark.
These are promises to keep moving,
to let hope guide me when days are dim.
In the moon's soft glow, I feel my strength,
a quiet resolve to hold on, to believe.
The stars seem to nod in silent support,
encouraging dreams I barely speak.
With each breath under this midnight sky,
I renew my vow to stay, to rise,
to trust in hope, as constant as the moon.

Whispers to the Night

Under the moon's calm, knowing gaze,
I feel a peace that words can't name.
I make promises to the night itself,
vows of hope to carry into dawn.
The stars above seem to listen close,
a celestial choir, silent yet strong.
Here, under this sky, I dare to believe,
to hold onto dreams not yet seen.
In the moonlight, I release my fears,
letting hope settle deep within.
I vow to trust in what's still unknown,
to walk forward in gentle courage.
These moonlit promises are mine alone,
oaths I carry as I journey on,
guided by the quiet strength of night.

Vows Beneath the Stars

With only the moon to witness my vow,
I make a promise beneath the stars.
To remain hopeful through every storm,
to hold onto light when shadows grow.
The sky above, a vast and silent friend,
seems to understand these hidden dreams.
I find comfort in the night's embrace,
a quiet strength that steadies my heart.
Each star feels like a wordless reminder,
a gentle nudge to keep on, to believe.
Under this sky, I vow to stay strong,
to rise with hope as constant as the stars.
In the moon's glow, I make a silent pledge,
a promise that needs no witness but night,
a vow to find light, even in the dark.

The Rhythm of Return

The waves arrive, as they always do,
no words needed, no grand declarations.
Each surge a promise to return again,
a silent oath woven into the tides.
They come with strength, with gentle grace,
greeting the shore in eternal rhythm.
No voice needed, no sign to be shown—
the ocean's promise is steadfast, true.
Each wave carries a vow, deep and calm,
a trust that this dance will never cease.
Through storms and stillness, it holds steady,
a bond of water and earth, soft yet sure.
The shore waits, knowing this promise well,
a silent trust in each rising swell,
as waves return, faithful as breath.

A Promise Worn Smooth

Each wave that touches the waiting sand
speaks in a language older than words.
The ocean promises without a sound,
its return as sure as the dawn's light.
There is no need for spoken vows—
its rhythm is truth, a pledge of faith.
The waves recede, but always return,
bearing witness to their own constancy.
In every crest and gentle break,
a silent promise flows to the shore,
a reminder that change can be steady,
a bond unbroken by distance or time.
We find peace in its wordless refrain,
the endless coming back, back again,
a whispered vow told only in waves.

The Ocean's Oath

Without a single word or sound,
the ocean pledges itself to return.
Each wave a promise made and kept,
a bond woven in currents and tides.
The shore waits patiently, calm, assured,
knowing the ocean will not stray far.
Its ebb and flow a timeless agreement,
a vow repeated by each rising swell.
There is comfort in this steady dance,
in the quiet promise that comes and goes.
No need to wonder if it will keep—
the waves arrive, faithful, constant.
The ocean's oath is as old as stone,
an unspoken vow to never stay away,
a promise that holds as the world turns.

A Wordless Assurance

The ocean meets the shore in silence,
yet its presence speaks in endless waves.
Each return is a promise renewed,
a vow whispered by the tide's embrace.
No words are needed, no spoken bond,
just the quiet rhythm of approach and retreat.
This is a love ancient and profound,
a trust that deepens with each gentle crash.
The waves arrive, then pull away,
but never do they truly leave.
Each crest carries a silent assurance,
a reminder of nature's constant promise.
The shore trusts in this quiet oath,
in the silent return that never fails,
a bond of water and earth, forever entwined.

Unbroken Cycles

In silence, the seasons shift and change,
an eternal dance that needs no sound.
Spring arrives with buds that gently bloom,
followed by summer's sunlit warmth.
Then autumn breathes its golden hues,
and winter settles, soft and still.
Nature moves through each stage unfaltering,
a quiet promise to rise and renew.
There's no need for words or explanations;
its cycle is faithful, its rhythm true.
Through storms, droughts, and silent nights,
the seasons turn with timeless grace.
It is nature's way of keeping faith,
a vow as old as earth and air,
to bloom, to fade, to rise again.

The Quiet Turning

Without words, the earth unfolds its promise,
a cycle unbroken, deeply known.
Each season returns in silence strong,
a testament to life's quiet resolve.
Spring brings life, a soft rebirth,
while summer follows, bold and bright.
Then autumn whispers its amber song,
and winter falls in muted white.
No matter what the world may face,
the seasons keep their ancient course,
a silent commitment to move and change,
to give and rest, to grow and fade.
Nature's resilience speaks without words,
a reminder of strength in quiet things,
a vow that time cannot erase.

The Promise of Return

In the stillness, nature holds its vow,
a silent promise woven in time.
Seasons turn, as they always will,
each one a chapter, a steady refrain.
Spring arrives, bringing hope anew,
summer glows with warm embrace,
autumn colors the world in fire and rust,
while winter blankets all in quiet rest.
This is the earth's unspoken pledge—
to keep moving, to keep renewing,
a cycle held in gentle trust,
unwavering, calm, and endlessly true.
No matter what storms may come,
nature commits to rise once more,
its wordless faith woven into the land.

Endurance in Silence

In every leaf, in every breeze,
nature holds a quiet resolve.
It does not need to speak or explain,
for its promise is written in each turn.
Spring will awaken the earth once more,
summer will follow with green abundance,
autumn will breathe in fire and calm,
and winter will cradle the world in rest.
Seasons come as surely as breath,
unfazed by circumstance or change.
This cycle is nature's steadfast pledge,
a silent oath to endure and renew.
With each shift, the earth reaffirms
its ancient promise to begin again,
a testament to strength held in silence.

Whispers of the Stars

The stars shimmer with unspoken truths,
silent promises woven in light.
They watch over us from distant realms,
holding mysteries beyond our reach.
Each night, they shine with patient grace,
as if they know a future yet unseen.
We look to them, seeking meaning,
drawn to the secrets they quietly keep.
Their light travels across endless miles,
carrying whispers of what may come.
Though we cannot grasp their distant plans,
we feel their presence, timeless and calm.
In their glow lies a silent vow,
a promise that spans the bounds of time,
guiding us forward, though we know not where.

Promises in the Night Sky

Above us, stars hang like ancient words,
messages sent through boundless dark.
They do not explain their quiet purpose,
yet we feel their promise, vast and deep.
Each star is a seed of something unknown,
a glimpse of futures waiting to bloom.
We gaze at them, sensing hidden truths,
drawn by a faith we can't explain.
They are keepers of cosmic dreams,
guardians of paths we have yet to find.
The future hums in their steady light,
a promise to hold us as we seek.
These stars, so silent, so far away,
carry the weight of mysteries unspoken,
whispers of what we will one day know.

A Cosmic Pledge

In the quiet of night, stars glow soft,
a constant reminder of distant hope.
They are promises suspended in space,
vows of futures we cannot yet touch.
With every shimmer, they hint at more,
at destinies yet unseen, unknown.
Their light reaches us across time,
a silent message waiting to unfold.
We look to them with awe and wonder,
sensing their truth, though it remains hidden.
Each star holds a part of the future's map,
a guide drawn in constellations bright.
Though we may not grasp their purpose now,
the cosmos holds us in its endless care,
promising to reveal itself in time.

Guardians of Tomorrow

The stars, like lanterns in endless dark,
watch over us with a quiet strength.
They hold secrets woven in stardust,
promises sealed in the fabric of time.
Each one carries a future unseen,
a destiny crafted far from reach.
They remain, patient and steadfast,
guiding us with a silent vow.
We stare up, sensing their ancient truth,
a knowledge deep and just beyond grasp.
They are guardians of what will come,
keepers of paths not yet revealed.
Their light is a promise, vast and calm,
a gentle guide through life's unknowns,
assuring us that we are not alone.

Disclaimer

This book, Unspoken Promises, is a work of creative expression. The poems within are inspired by universal themes of love, relationships, self-reflection, and connection but are entirely fictional and intended for emotional and artistic exploration. Any resemblance to real persons, living or deceased, or to specific events is purely coincidental.

The themes explored in this collection may evoke personal reflections or memories; however, they are not meant to offer professional advice, therapy, or guidance. Readers are encouraged to seek appropriate support if they find any content emotionally challenging.

Unspoken Promises is meant to be an artistic journey into the subtleties of unspoken connections, offering readers a safe space for introspection and the exploration of silent emotions. Enjoy the experience with an open heart, and may these poems bring comfort and resonance in their quiet way.